FIVE DAYS, FIVE NIGHTS

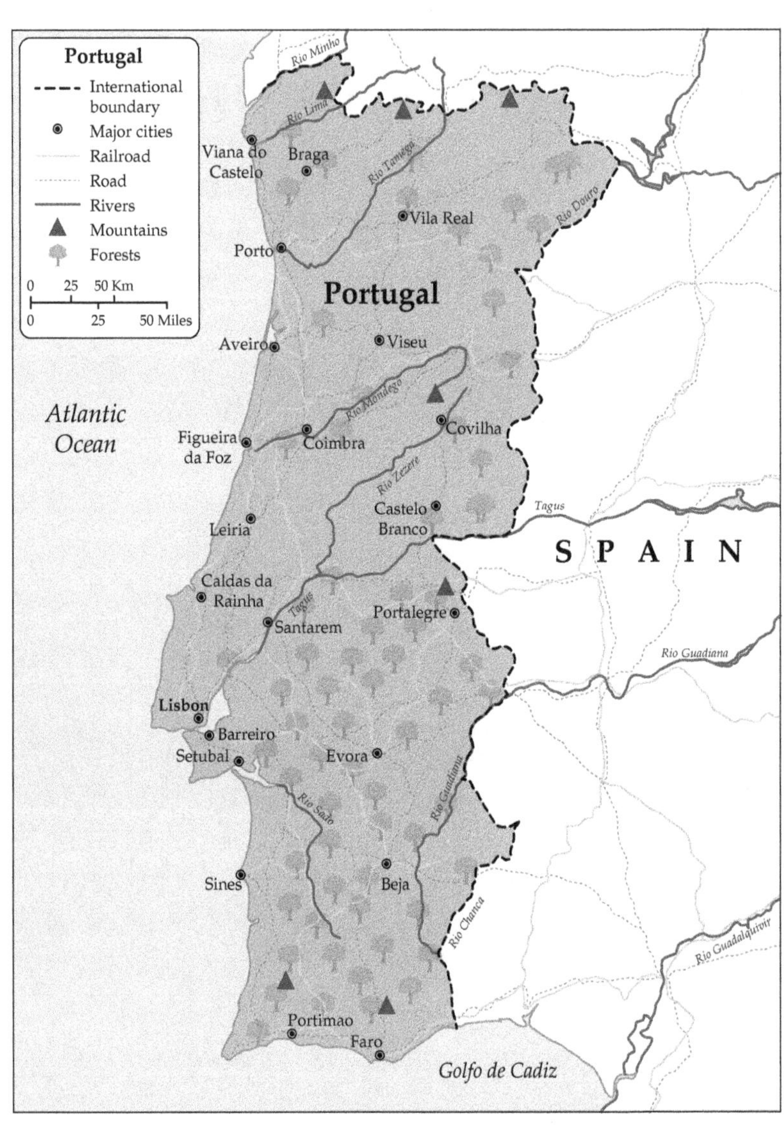

Portugal
International boundary
Major cities
Railroad
Road
Rivers
Mountains
Forests
0   25   50 Km
0   25   50 Miles
Atlantic Ocean
Rio Minho
Rio Lima
Rio Tamega
Rio Douro
Viana do Castelo
Braga
Vila Real
Porto
Portugal
Aveiro
Viseu
Rio Mondego
Covilha
Figueira da Foz
Coimbra
Rio Zezere
Tagus
Leiria
Castelo Branco
SPAIN
Caldas da Rainha
Tagus
Portalegre
Santarem
Rio Guadiana
Lisbon
Barreiro
Setubal
Evora
Rio Sado
Rio Guadiana
Sines
Beja
Rio Chanca
Rio Guadalquivir
Portimao
Faro
Golfo de Cadiz

FIVE DAYS, FIVE NIGHTS

(Cinco Dias, Cinco Noites)

MANUEL TIAGO
(ALVARO CUNHAL)

Translated and with a foreword by
ERIC A. GORDON
Illustrations by Ilse Gordon

INTERNATIONAL PUBLISHERS, New York

First English language edition, 2020 by International Publishers Co., Inc. / NY by special arrangement with Editorial Avante!

Translated from the Portuguese by Eric A. Gordon © 2019

Printed in the United States of America

Library of Congress Cataloging-in-Publication Data

Names: Tiago, Manuel, author. | Gordon, Eric A., 1945- translator.
Title: Five days, five nights = (Cinco dias, cinco noites) / Manuel Tiago
  (Alvaro Cunhal) ; translated and with a foreword by Eric A. Gordon ;
  illustrations by Ilse Gordon.
Other titles: Cinco dias, cinco noites. English
Description: First English language edition. | New York : International
  Publishers, 2020.
Identifiers: LCCN 2020012434 | ISBN 9780717807895 (paperback) |
  ISBN 0717807894 (paperback)
Classification: LCC PQ9282.I23 C5613 2020 | DDC 869.3/42—dc23
LC record available at https://lccn.loc.gov/2020012434

ISBN-10: 0-7178-0789-4   ISBN-13: 978-0-7178-0789-5
Typeset by Amnet Systems, Chennai, India

Table of Contents

Illustrations

Photos

Foreword

The Portuguese Communist Party is, proportionate to the size of the country's population, one of the largest in the world, certainly in the capitalist world. It must have come as something of a surprise for Portuguese readers to learn that its longtime leader, Alvaro Cunhal, had made a sideline career for himself as a neorealist fiction writer. This book is the first to appear in English. International Publishers, renowned for its historic catalogue of publications of non-fiction, including Marxist theoretical studies, fiction, memoir and poetry, is proud to present this unusual novella as a long overdue expression of gratitude for Alvaro Cunhal's self-sacrificing leadership of the Portuguese Communists during most of the half-century of fascism in his land.

We are also pleased to discover a literary talent heretofore unknown in the English-reading world. Even in this short book, "Manuel Tiago" ranges far beyond the didactic, prosaic, expository style for which, alas, much political writing is (un)distinguished. Tiago's use of language is rich and exuberant, while still retaining the earthy authenticity of the vernacular. His characterizations are empathic and intuitive. Without bothering to recapitulate the class origins, family background or education of his characters, he leaves it to the reader to figure out just where and how these factors contribute to the story. Like a master painter, he supplies enough suggestive detail to fill out a larger picture of Portuguese society.

Stylistically, *Five Days, Five Nights* approximates something of the 1940s and '50s noir writers' and filmmakers' hyper-realist sensibilities, though any direct influence on the writer is not likely, for Cunhal wrote this book while imprisoned in Portugal in the 1950s. He was able to slip it past the censors, who saw little specifically political in it, merely the story of an emigrant escaping the country, a common occurrence at the time. Notably, there is no reference to the Party as such, though readers are welcome to infer its presence in the background.

The manuscript of this novella was found in the archives of the Forte de Peniche, where Cunhal had been imprisoned. Cunhal had left it behind when he escaped on January 3, 1960, although he did take with him the manuscript to another, much longer and more specifically political novel, *Até Amanhã, Camaradas*. After the 25th of April 1974 Revolution that brought an end to fascism in Portugal, the military officers in charge of the fort returned the manuscript to Cunhal, and he published it in 1975 under the pseudonym Manuel Tiago, with a fictitious indication that it had been found in the "author's" papers after his death (an explanation he also used for *Até Amanhã, Camaradas*).

The true authorship of these books was known to the Party leadership. Only later in life, in 1994, did Cunhal acknowledge that he was "Manuel Tiago," pseudonymous author of several books (whose titles are noted here in the biography of the author).

Cunhal had obviously heard many stories of his comrades' clandestine emigration across the border. Possibly, too, there may be some autobiographical content to the story.

As for the time frame of the story, there is no reference to telephones (available even into the 1950s only in post offices and in wealthier homes), nor even telegraphs, which were expensive and used only in emergency situations. Yet there are trains and motor vehicles that connected cities and reached into some backward rural areas. There is also no reference made to any world events, not even to the existence of a socialist Soviet Union, although writing in prison, of course, Cunhal had to be cautious of the state security censorship.

Given the author's involvement in the Portuguese student movement based in Lisbon in the very early years of António Salazar's Estado Novo—a "New State" version of fascism—a setting of early 1930s would seem probable. Furthermore, it seems to predate the Spanish Civil War (1936-39) and Francisco Franco's subsequent fascist regime if we are to accept the logic of an escape over the border from oppressive

Portugal to the untroubled Spain described in the book. We do not know, however, if the refugee's ultimate destination was Spain. Perhaps even during the civil war, he might have intended to pass through Spain to France, the USSR, or some other place.

If we understand the story as existing outside of a specific time, however, involving archetypal situations, relationships and circumstances, then to that extent it achieves a certain universality, standing in for similar, parallel conditions almost anywhere in the world at any time.

Five Days, Five Nights is largely devoid of political speechifying, but it is hardly without political and social significance. Without giving his readers much of a backstory to his characters, he nevertheless portrays the world of urban intellectuals and how detached their lives can be from the experience of activists and militants and the ordinary dwellers of rural areas. He depicts a traditional, undeveloped countryside— and perhaps by extension a country—in isolation from the main currents of progress and technology in the world. The Portugal he gives us is a poor, backwater land whose prospects can be improved only by more democracy. The more we understand about that Portugal, the more astounding it seems that nevertheless this small country possessed enough of a managerial and military class to remain among the largest colonial powers even well into the post-World War II era, with its far-reaching global empire in Africa and Asia. Maintenance of that empire cost the metropolis dearly.

Five Days, Five Nights surely was written to remind readers not only of the sacrifices made by fascism's resisters, but of the loss of creativity and intelligence that Portugal suffered by its erosion of talented, hardworking citizens.

The armed anti-colonialist movements in Angola, Mozambique and Guiné-Bissau, as well as elsewhere, began in the 1960s and inspired the domestic resistance to oppose Portugal's overseas imperial wars. Before that time, i.e., when this book was written, the colonial question had not been central to the antifascist resistance. The action of the Portuguese military to bring down the colonial-fascist regime in 1974 was a conjunction of factors, among which the role of the Portuguese Communist Party in its long struggle against both fascism and colonialism was decisive. The defeat of the fascist regime after almost 50 years is yet another example that tyranny cannot last forever.

Eric A. Gordon, January 2020

FIVE DAYS, FIVE NIGHTS

Lambaça and André each tried to figure out what kind of man he was dealing with.

From the posthumous papers of "Manuel Tiago" found in a clandestine archive, together with the novel Até Amanhã, Camaradas ("Until Tomorrow, Comrades") and other original writings.

FIVE DAYS, FIVE NIGHTS
a novella
by Manuel Tiago
English translation by Eric A. Gordon

Chapter 1

JUST short of turning nineteen, André was forced to emigrate. They raised money for him, they gave him an address in Porto, and they told him passage would be worked out for him across the border to Spain. However, things were not so simple. In Porto, the people he was referred to swore straightaway there was nothing they could do. Only after two nerve-racking weeks of waiting did they wind up pointing him toward one Lambaça, a smuggler, who said he could take André to Spain for a thousand escudos. Then they warned:

"The guy has a track record for trouble—knife fights. And robbery, too, so it seems. It's a poor solution, but we don't see any other. You decide."

André made up his mind and was brought to meet the man.

The encounter took place near the Campanhã station, at a deserted spot some distance from the city in the wee hours of the day. It was dark and humid, warmish and windless. After sneaking along the length of a fence, over which they could hear the metallic clang of switching railcars, André and the comrade who was going to introduce him turned on to the tracks. They continued a hundred meters or so and stopped abruptly. Out of the silent darkness, the glow of a cigarette shone from a few feet away.

"The train's already gone," said the comrade obliquely.

As if in response, the little fire from the cigarette winked three times in the dark. They moved closer. The figure of the smoker came into better focus as he approached them also.

"This is our friend," the comrade said, not clarifying if he meant the smoker or André.

André grasped a rough, bony, strong hand. Now close to him, once again the light from the cigarette flared. André guessed he saw a black mustache and a brown, angular face.

The three figures descended the slope alongside the railway and continued down a shadowy trail squeezed between rows of unkempt trees. A vague, sweet smell of oil clung to the air. Once again, suddenly, but now from a greater distance, they could hear the isolated sound of switching rail cars.

Farther on, they halted. Turning to face one another, Lambaça and André each tried to figure out what kind of man he was dealing with. In the dark, however, they couldn't discern a thing.

It was the next day, when they met again, that they got to know one another. Somewhere between forty and fifty, Lambaça, short and wizened, had a cheerless face of a strong brown color, accentuated by a thick growth of whiskers, a black brush mustache, and small, dark, attentive eyes. By his dress, a wrinkled, tight-fitting black suit with a black hat resting on his eyebrows, you would say he was a common laborer in his Sunday best. But in the totality of his physique, in the erectness of his torso and the way he deployed his legs, in his gestures and his watchfulness, he manifested something that distinguished him from ordinary men, something arrogant, daring and insolent.

André was short, too, thin and dark. With an uncovered head, his hair tumbled over his forehead. His worried expression only called attention to his youth.

Each of them took a sharp disliking toward the other. To Lambaça, who imagined he'd be helping some important leader cross the border, André appeared to be an insignificant, innocent child, rendering his mission almost ridiculous.

Lambaça's appearance and demeanor only exacerbated the mistrust and caution André already felt.

"This can be done," Lambaça pronounced in a disdainful, authoritarian voice, measuring the young man disparagingly from head to toe. "Are you used to walking, my friend? Because we're going to be trekking some good long distances."

André reassured him he was up to it.

"Good," Lambaça stated. "It's not only that. I don't know you at all, and this stuff is for men. I'll put you on the other side with no trouble, but you need to be tough."

"Don't worry," André answered.

Lambaça quickened his pace. They walked a while without talking, and André saw that the other man was not going to say anything further. With his burdened expression under the shadow of his black hat, you could say he didn't even notice he had company.

"When are we leaving?" André asked finally.

"When are we leaving?" Lambaça seemed to wake up. He stopped and looked at the young man in a mixture of surprise and mockery.

"Yes, when do we leave?"

Lambaça thought a while and in a slow, disinterested tone he set a date for three days from now, early in the morning.

"They told me it would be tomorrow," André said.

"People tell me a lot of things, too," Lambaça replied, shrugging his shoulders.

And adding nothing more, only making a slight gesture with his hand, which could be either a goodbye or a sign for the boy to wait, he disappeared into the door of a bar.

Not knowing how to interpret that behavior, André waited another few minutes. Finally, he decided to leave.

This isn't going to work, he thought. *He's not going to show up.*

By the time he was just a few steps away from the guardhouse, he found himself in the middle of the crowd.

Chapter 2

BUT he did show up. He appeared, and led André to a cheap tavern, where he ordered packages of bread and fried fish, and drank a glass of wine. He then purchased the train tickets and chose their carriage. He hardly spoke, but revealed no sense of annoyance or resentment.

They traveled several hours on the train, ate their lunch, and around midday got off in a bright, sunny little town. There they would catch a jitney that took a route toward the border. They began seeing security and needed to avoid danger. The jitney would pass through a town with a guardhouse. According to Lambaça, it was common for them to ask for passengers' documents there. Lambaça explained his plan in the tone of one who gives orders, since in truth that's what he was giving.

"Here's what we'll do. We'll have the jitney stop before it reaches the guardhouse. You get out and walk ahead casually. You'll actually pass by the guardhouse door. Going on foot, the police will think you're just visiting somewhere in the area and won't say anything to you. Continue following the road as quickly as you can, but not running. The jitney will stop at the guardhouse, they'll check us out, and when we catch up to you, I'll have it stop and pick you up."

To André, all this sounded rather unsafe and risky.

"At the guardhouse, they'll let me walk past?" he asked. "And won't the other passengers and the driver wonder—"

"Leave it to me," Lambaça cut him off.

For an instant, the young man thought of saying goodbye to the smuggler and taking the train back the other way. He didn't, but only because of the cunning look those shining black eyes gave him. *It looks like you're afraid!* those eyes said.

Waiting for the jitney to depart, Lambaça brought his companion to a tavern and started drinking. A troubled André did not sit down with him and went to the door, looking out. Lambaça appeared not to see him. Propped up at the counter, he tasted the wine in little sips, and with a slow gesture, wiped off his mustache every time with the bony back of his hand. With his eyes half-closed, he looked sleepy and inattentive.

They got into the jitney, which sluggishly, jerkily followed a dusty, rutted road. It stopped here and there in doleful, peaceable townships, where peasants of few words got on and got off. André, who was born and had always lived in Lisbon, observed both the landscape and the people with curiosity. He admired the young girls, helped to unload their baskets and, when looking directly at other people, one could read in his honest eyes a barely restrained desire to talk and socialize. At his side, tall and rigid, Lambaça smoked cigarette after cigarette without saying a word.

Unexpectedly, Lambaça pulled the bell cord and elbowed his companion. *Now*, André figured.

The jitney stopped and André stepped down. He saw a row of houses on one side, and on the other, just below, some fifty meters away, a group of people looking at the jitney and at him. *The guardhouse*, he thought. The jitney started moving again and slowly continued in the same direction. *Is this guy crazy or what?* André asked himself. *This is like playing a secret game in full view of the enemy.* The jitney went on, the crowd of people continued looking in his direction, and amongst them André picked out two fellows with city clothes and shining hair, raising their heads with curiosity.

What stupidity! What stupidity! he thought. The jitney passed him by and stopped in front of the guardhouse. André was only about twenty meters away. Should he cross the road and continue walking, blocked from view by the jitney? Or go on and melt into the group, meekly excusing himself to pass through or elbowing the policemen themselves? He didn't have time to decide. By the time he was just a few steps away from the guardhouse, he found himself in the middle of the crowd. Without knowing why, he made a show of greeting a little girl with a friendly "hello," and in that moment, at his side and staring at him, he saw the inquisitive face of one of the agents. He elbowed his way through a group of three peasants, and as he passed the guardhouse and the jitney, felt an intense impulse to run. But he assumed the policeman's eyes would be following him, so in no hurry, with a relaxed ease that gave him a strange pleasure, he pretended to adjust his shoelace. He looked around at the houses, as if recognizing the place, and then casually left. With each step, slow and apparently innocent, he expected to hear at his side a commanding "Halt!" and all would be lost. But no. He distanced himself, the houses thinned out, the road curved to the right, putting him out of view of the guardhouse, and nothing out of the ordinary happened.

When he saw he was away from the settlement, remembering what Lambaça had told him, he stepped up his pace, almost running. He followed the road a good two kilometers, always expecting to hear the jitney behind him. Nothing. On the silent, sunny road, not a living soul could be seen.

The curves described a long ascent, foretelling deserted mountains ahead. The jitney's delay began to disturb him. Would it really come out this far? Or was the guy playing a trick on him? Could that maneuver at the guardhouse have been an attempt to turn him in, protecting Lambaça himself against any accusation?

Walking another kilometer along the deserted road, he stopped, panting and discouraged. He had just sat down by the wayside when the sound of an engine rumbled nearby and the jitney rounded the last curve, followed by a plume of dust glistening in the sun. André jumped to the road. Finally!

The jitney drew near, rising uphill and coughing, but when it got to André, it barely slowed down: It continued on, chugging up ahead. André thought he saw an arm signaling from a window. A cloud of dust covered and suffocated him. The snort of the motor could be heard for a long time, rising, rising, declaring the ruggedness of the mountains. André felt humiliated, thrown into a trap. He called himself stupid and naïve, and in that moment, with nothing else clear in his brain, he felt a burning hatred for Lambaça.

Did he really see an arm from the window giving a sign that he follow? Was it Lambaça? Or someone throwing a fruit peel? Or just feeling the weight of the air? He couldn't say. But before he could reflect on it any further, his body answered the appeal of that arm, real or imaginary. And he ran up the hill, overheated and out of breath, behind the roaring vehicle, which disappeared into the distance.

Chapter 3

HE found Lambaça in a bar on a narrow little street, drinking. André had run and walked more than ten kilometers to town, gone into bar after bar, and now here he was, dripping sweat, staring silent and raging at his companion. *You didn't wait for me, eh? Well, you can't get rid of me like that!* he seemed to say.

Lambaça made a slight gesture of surprise, which he shortly suppressed. He slowly finished drinking his glass, cleaned the brush of his black mustache with the back of his hand and drew the young man closer to him. The police had asked for everyone's documents. One of them rode along in the jitney. It was impossible to ask it to stop.

André answered him in a sharp, angry voice. If that was the case, why didn't he join him? And why did he go plant himself in a bar on this out-of-the-way street? What kind of confidence did he inspire?

Lambaça stared at him a few seconds with his surly eyes. Then, without responding, he shrugged his shoulders and started rolling a cigarette with a deliberation obviously feigned by those bony, unsteady fingers.

"So in the end what are you thinking?" a furious André continued. "Are you regretting the deal you made? Are you afraid now? Or do you want more money?"

Lambaça raised his eyes from the tobacco he was rolling and peered back unresponsively. In his gaze were threat, derision and something else, different and indecipherable. He finished rolling the cigarette and lit it.

"It's better if we went to have a bite to eat," he said.

They both devoured their platter of cod and chickpeas. Dehydrated from all the running, André drank several glasses of water, and Lambaça as many of wine. He was visibly affected by the alcohol: His reddened eyes laughed provocatively every time his companion raised his glass of water to his lips. Without removing his hat, he removed his black jacket, revealing, in his pocket, well within André's line of vision, an enormous silver revolver. His overstretched suspenders tugged at his shirt, allowing his muscular shoulders to be seen. Only at the end of the meal did he break the silence. His voice, thickened by the wine, was even more jeering and arrogant.

"I want to answer your question of a while ago, my friend. My thinking is this: A thousand escudos isn't much." The small ironic eyes did not leave André's face. "Two thousand, is that good?"

Scoundrel! André thought. "You'll get two thousand," he said.

"And you have them?"

The young man's face screwed up with anger. His hand reached across the table and grabbled Lambaça's sinewy, hairy wrist.

"Who do you think you're dealing with? Or is it the drink that makes you talk like that?"

They looked at each other with loathing. Then, Lambaça's loose hand grabbed André's and firmly freed his wrist.

"You have them?" he repeated.

André reached into his pocket, pulled out an envelope and opened it. It was evidently more than the amount demanded.

Lambaça had a disagreeable smile, smelling of wine and exposing his dark, rotten teeth.

"Good. Agreed. Two thousand."

Chapter 4

BY the time they left the tavern, night was falling. Lambaça led his companion through narrow, old streets filled with the bittersweet smell of cooking rye. They left the village on a rocky lane, which descended tortuously between trellises and walls. A few peasants, returning from work, passed them and greeted them placidly. At the end of the lane, gurgling between weeds and river stones, ran a stream so fresh you could breathe it in. For a long time, in the dark now, Lambaça guided his companion alongside the stream, cutting through the foliage, scrambling up from the water's edge and then back to it. He pushed aside shrubs, warned about holes and rubble and, like a black eel, slipped through high, almost impenetrable thickets. He seemed bent on demonstrating to André that despite being soaked in wine, he knew this terrain like the back of his hand. From time to time, he stopped, but not out of uncertainty. Standing, his compact, stiff, bristly body turned slowly in the dark, his head rotating from one side to the other, like an animal sniffing out danger. Then he proceeded with confidence.

Having left the village more than three hours before, they stopped in an open, earthy field. A sudden breath of wind caressed their sweaty skin. Lambaça sat himself down on a mound and started rolling a cigarette.

"Did we cross?" André asked.

Lambaça finished making his cigarette and lit it with a bright red match flame that irritated his eyes. He took a few draws of smoke and only then laughed with a dry, forced guffaw. He did not respond.

It was evident they had not crossed. More and more, André felt less and less confident of this man. What was he scheming?

"Will we cross tonight?" he corrected himself.

Lambaça drew again on his smoke, and in the reddish light André thought he saw those black eyes peering at him with evil intent.

"These things don't happen that way, my friend," he said in a condescending voice.

"Where do we sleep? Here?"

He felt tired and sleepy. Running behind the jitney had left a sharp pang at the bottom of his lung.

He sensed that Lambaça was shrugging his shoulders.

"Leave it to me," he answered.

"No, my friend," André replied. "Now it's me saying that things cannot continue this way. I don't like walking blind, and I shouldn't have to. What is your plan?"

"Quiet, keep your voice down," Lambaça counseled paternalistically.

And he remained silent, sucking now and again on his cigarette in the same sensuous way he had drunk the wine.

"So? What is your plan?" said André in a lower voice, but without disguising his extreme impatience.

Only after a while did Lambaça answer, and slowly.

"There's still plenty of time to turn back."

Turn back? Turn back all alone, in a completely unfamiliar borderland region, where with every step one could only guess at the danger from a bad encounter? Lambaça knew he had the boy at his disposal, and smugly enjoyed it.

André did not give in, however. He spoke of the importance of the crossing, of responsibilities, cooperation. Now he spoke with a calm, persuasive voice, and leaning forward, attempted to discern in Lambaça some expression or gesture.

In the dark of the night, Lambaça, still as a stone, did not react. Only when André had finished did he say, his words drawling with contempt, "I've known all that for more than twenty years."

Having said that, he removed his jacket and, placing it on the ground, opened the whiteness of his shirt to the night. The metal of his revolver glinted as he adjusted it to his waist. He walked away without saying anything and returned only much later.

The woman crushed the length of silk violently, threw it on the floor and stepped on it repeatedly in her wooden clogs.

Chapter 5

IT couldn't have been much before midnight when they approached a dark house somewhere in the deserted countryside. Inside the house, a woman was screaming angrily. A dog barked. A door higher up on the porch revealed a yellow rectangle of light in which the black outline of a figure shortly appeared.

"Douro!"

The dog growled, then went quiet. The voice of the woman who had been yelling inside escaped from the house out of control.

They went up the stairs.

"Ah! It's you!" said the woman opening the door. She was a fat, old woman, cloaked in an enormous black shawl. "Come in."

Upon entering, they immediately saw the screaming woman. She didn't turn when they entered or respond to their greeting. Next to a sewing machine, wriggling in her chair as if she were on hot coals, the woman held a magnificent length of blue silk while she continued to shriek.

"For what? What's this for? He's mocking me! Ah! But he'll be sorry, yeah, very sorry. I'm cutting him loose, and when he least expects it! Always, always, always, always, this nastiness! Just to be difficult! Just to do mean stuff!"

The woman turned toward the older one, looking past the visitors without seeing them. For a moment, her face shone in the light of the oil lamp. She was inflamed and disheveled, her headscarf fallen to her shoulders, her enraged eyes appearing like shining beads, her mouth foaming beneath the visible hairs on her upper lip.

"Look at this! Just look at this!" and she held out the length of silk to the old lady. "I'm giving it to him right to his face! Yes I am!"

"Really," the old woman said indifferently.

"He could have said no right away. It would have been nicer." Using a falsetto voice to imitate someone, and laughing maniacally, she continued, "No, sir! Honey here, honey there. He got me, yes he did, but he won't fool me again! As you do, you must pay! I'd be the stupidest of the stupid if you don't pay me!"

"Really," the old woman said again.

"Ah, no! No way! No, no, no and no! Do you want to dance? So dance, my dear, you'll see if you can dance or can't dance! You ain't seen nothing yet! But you will see it! Oh, yes you will! Honey? What about that, honey? I'll give you honey! Take this! Take this! Take this! Take this!"

Shouting like that, the woman crushed the length of silk violently, threw it on the floor and stepped on it repeatedly in her wooden clogs. They appeared brutish and enormous in the light.

What a witch! thought André, still overcome by surprise.

After this outburst, the woman quieted down and calmed herself. She arranged her hair and her scarf, cleaned off her mouth with a dark cloth taken from a pocket in her apron, and started straightening out some clothes on the sewing machine. Only then did she notice the visitors.

"Have you been there?" she said to Lambaça in a voice still trembling with anger. "There's no charge to sit down."

The old woman lifted the silk off the floor and began cleaning it off and smoothing it out.

Hardly had they sat down when they heard steps on the stone staircase. The door opened and two men entered unhurriedly. They spoke to Lambaça as someone they knew and observed André with a fixed gaze. Without removing their hats, like Lambaça, they remained standing next to the table, their faces illuminated from below by the oil lamp. One had a rough, masculine face with a deep scar on one cheek; the other was young, with a pale face, worried and cold.

The one with the scar watched the old woman attentively as she cleaned and smoothed the length of silk. She cocked her head toward the other woman. She continued to organize pieces of clothing on top of the sewing machine, but clearly she was doing so not out of necessity but to avoid looking at the visitors.

"So?" asked the scarred man, directing himself to her.

The old lady touched him on the arm and raised a finger to her nose. The man remained impassive.

"Coffee?" she asked, turning to Lambaça.

He shook his head to say no and silently looked at André. The two men and the old woman looked at one another. The other woman turned to look at him too. André felt deeply uncomfortable. The envelope with the money in his pocket unnerved him.

"How are things here?" Lambaça asked.

"So-so…," the scarface answered.

They stayed quiet several minutes. The scar-faced man disappeared through a door and returned shortly after. Without saying anything, Lambaça rose and went out to the porch. Scarface followed, closing the door behind him.

For a good long while, André followed the movements of the woman at the sewing machine as she rearranged the articles of clothing without purpose. The old woman, still smoothing the silk, and the younger man, with his hand poised on the edge of the oil lamp, watched him sideways, seriously and distrustingly.

"It's summer," André said, opening his shirt collar wider.

The old lady nodded. They continued in silence.

Chapter 6

THE young visitor exited by a warped back door that creaked when opened. The old woman fell asleep propped on the table. At the sewing machine, turned now toward the light, the other woman sewed wordlessly. André couldn't make out her face. As her face was obscured by the shadow of her headscarf, he caught the glint in her eyes only once in a while. She would look in his direction, then turn quickly away. He retained the image of the woman's face disfigured by rage and experienced a vague displeasure of spending the night with this harridan. Only the woman's hands surprised him. They were dainty, fair hands, whose fingers moved expertly and capably over her sewing.

Around one in the morning Lambaça returned with the scarface, who now brought a kerosene lantern that he placed on the table. He started to light it after removing the glass funnel from the oil lamp. The light dimmed and cast a reddish pall on the scene. The man's face, lit from below by the flickering flame, possessed something of the fantastic and sinister.

André looked at Lambaça, waiting for an explanation.

"We need to get some sleep," said Lambaça, answering the look on André's face.

He said no more, but the mocking tone of his voice added: *Patience, my boy, you don't need to know any more.*

"Over here," said the man with the scar.

André left with him and went out onto the porch.

"Are you staying?" he asked Lambaça, who was leaning on the table and slowly rolling a cigarette.

"Staying." Snide, cruel superiority was implied in this single word.

They descended the stairs. As they rounded the house, they walked along a path strewn with straw and manure and headed toward another building. In the darkness of the night, the dim, reddish glow of the lantern danced in front of André. It hovered over the earth like an enigma suspended midair in a gentle, rhythmic cadence. It faintly lit the man's pants and boots, which seemed to move without a body.

The lantern suddenly brought into view a few rungs of a wooden ladder leaning against a wall.

"Here," said Scarface, starting to mount the ladder.

The ladder led through a narrow passage and into a wide-open space at the top of the house. The man and the lantern went ahead, and André followed. Bent over, the man raised the lantern to the level of his head. André proceeded, curved over as well, feeling the low incline of the roof's crossbeams and thatch. The wooden floor, which gave a little under their feet, was covered by straw and earth. Farther on, in the semi-darkness, the straw was piled up into mounds.

"Sleep well," the man said.

The red light, lowered again to the level of the man's knee, went skipping away until it met the doorpost of the passage-way, where it halted. Hidden by the dim, inconstant shadow, it suddenly went out. Then André could only imagine a face near the floor, as he heard the movement of the man lowering himself down the ladder.

André remained alone in the dark. After a few minutes, he could make out the rectangle of light from the opening that led outside and, feeling his way along the floor and the roof, he drew closer to it. The opening had neither doorjamb nor gate. Only the night closed in upon it, with its smell of wet foliage. Nothing could be perceived distinctly. Blurry volumes could be trees as easily as houses. He could clearly hear the rhythmic, fleeting chirr of the wings of some unfamiliar insect.

He woke up in a fright. Someone was there, very close. Slight, intermittent sounds of straw surrendering to weight, along with other brief, indeterminate sounds and almost imperceptible movements, all indicated that this person was on his feet, awake and active. André moved his hand to his pocket: The envelope was there.

"Lambaça?" he asked.

No response. He stood up in one jump and leaned against the wall.

"If you don't answer I'm going to shoot!" he threatened.

He was not armed, but he said it without thinking.

"Yes, it's me," answered Lambaça in an irked voice coming from above, muffled by the thatching on the roof. "None of this bull."

André heard more scuffling on the straw, then the same almost imperceptible sounds. Finally, Lambaça's boots hit the floor with little squeaks, making it quiver slightly. For a moment, the faint rectangle of the opening to the outside disappeared. Soon, whispering voices could be heard.

Finally, just at dawn, he fell asleep.

Chapter 7

HE waited a long time for something more to happen. Finally, just at dawn, he fell asleep. When he awoke again, chilly and exhausted, a ray of sun lit up the edge of the attic opening. The envelope with the money was in his pocket. The bag he had brought, with papers, clothes and a safety razor, was there too, intact. As he peeked out a cool, clear air bathed him, drenched with morning dew. A few steps away, he saw the back of the house with the loose gravel. In the courtyard, piles of straw pointed skyward. Beyond the house, naked, rounded mountains opened up, flattened out by the sun that sweetly softened them out. All breathed calm and harmony.

Grabbing his bag, he descended the wooden ladder and circled around the house. The dog jumped up barking.

"Douro!"—now in a crisp woman's voice coming from the porch.

The dog hushed, and he walked up the stairs. The woman, who the night before had been attacking the silk, sat next to the sewing machine as if she had not moved from there all night. Neither Lambaça, nor the man with the scar, nor the younger man, nor the old lady was there. But the woman who shushed the dog casually let him in and told him to have a seat. The other woman did not turn around.

"My companion?" André asked.

"He's coming," answered a thin, wet voice coming from the back of the room.

Only then did André notice an old man, whom he had not seen the night before, either. He was amiably laughing to himself.

"The village is far," the old man said. "Tired?"

"I slept well," André lied.

The woman who quieted the dog brought him bread, sausage and a pot of coffee. In her animated face that showed traces of nobility, a pair of honest eyes looked at him with curiosity.

"So young!" she remarked.

With those words, André realized that they knew everything.

The old man uttered a word, then another, alert and communicative. To each word of his own or André's, he stirred on his seat, moved his hands across his knees and responded readily to every turn of the conversation, expressing himself with extremely changeable moods of happiness, sadness, shock, questioning and doubt. The old man kept talking on and on, as if the first exchanges about the mountains and the town only meant to prepare the ground. In the end, only he spoke.

"The second time I went there was one of the saddest days of my life. I had gone to look for my shotgun. I sat myself down on the last step of the staircase and was setting up my things to clean it. My older daughter, who was seven then, wouldn't leave me alone. She wanted to play and wouldn't let me be. She kept coming at me, hitting me on my shoulder or arm and challenging me before running off laughing. 'Hey, you rascal, if I catch you, I'm going to kill you!' I said to her, and reached my hand over to the shotgun. She stopped a few steps away, paused, then came back very meekly, with the air of a saint, slowly she came closer and closer, and bam! Another hit with a shoe and she ran away laughing. 'Oh, you rascal, I'm gonna kill you!' I shouted, and raised my hand for the shotgun. She did that three, four, five times. Then it happened. An accident, just pure bad luck, but you must believe that I had left the weapon unloaded. Someone messed with it! No one admitted it, but someone messed with it! I would never have done that with a loaded gun. Someone messed with it!"

In the sudden excitement of telling the story, even at the distance of so many years, the old man recalled the violent accusations that people leveled against him.

"It was a terrible accident, and even today just remembering it makes me tremble. I picked up the shotgun and hardly touched it when *Booom!* The girl was standing three steps away from me, her shocked little face pouring blood. There was shouting everywhere, people came one by one, and there I am with her in my arms, running toward the town. My son Armando was saying, 'It's nothing, father, it's just some shotgun pellets, half a dozen if that. Don't you see it's a little thing?' Now, in truth, the girl was in perfect control of her senses, and what she said, my man! How could a child of that age, all gushing blood, speak like that? 'Don't be scared, daddy, don't be scared, it can't be anything.' She was consoling me—she, poor thing—with her little face, her hands, a leg, her dress, all red with blood. 'It wasn't your fault, daddy, I know it wasn't your fault,' she said. 'Don't be scared!' I ran as fast as I could through those mountains with her in my arms, until I got very tired and she noticed. 'Rest, daddy, you're very tired,' she said. So I rested a little, I cleaned her up once more, all the blood on her face and hands, and then stood up. 'Rest some more,' she insisted, 'rest.' 'No, my darling treasure,' I said, 'I don't want you to die, dear daughter.' And you know what that child responded? Seven years old, a child seven years old! She answered me like this: 'Never mind, don't be sorry, daddy, if I die, don't be sorry, nobody needs me, nobody will miss me.' And then how I cried, so much, so much, so much, so desperately, just remembering it brings back the same sorrow."

The old man stopped talking, his eyes brimming with tears, his lips trembling, unable to continue.

"And the girl died?" André asked.

Composing himself, the old man slowly blew his nose and wiped his face with a handkerchief, shaking his head.

"Look," he said. "That's her."

And he pointed with his sharp chin.

Immediately, André had empathized at once with the woman who shushed the dog, with her honest, friendly eyes and her animated, noble features. After that story from the old man, she appeared more sympathetic. He looked at her with renewed focus, trying to reconfigure her face as a child. The old man, however, captured the direction of André's glance and right away corrected him, already chuckling:

"Not her! The other one!"

The other one! The tender and courageous little girl was the "witch!"

To André's spirit came not the face convulsed by rage, but those fine, gentle hands that moved expertly and capably over the sewing.

Chapter **8**

LAMBAÇA, Scarface and the young lad showed up around midday, sweaty and silent. They did not say where they had been, and no one asked them. They hardly talked during lunch. Only the old man continued to babble while he chomped on his food with his bare gums and a single enormous tooth.

They took off after lunch. Gloomy, and sodden with wine, Lambaça headed for the mountains. His hat weighed heavily on him. Without turning toward his companion, he walked with long, slow steps of uninterrupted regularity. He didn't rest for hours.

Far from footpaths or settlements, the mountain wound around, stony and vacant. Only here and there, at the foot of a slope or behind a knoll, lay gentle specks of worked land. Who came to work them—and from where?—was a mystery in terrain so desolate and wild. All afternoon they walked, Lambaça ahead, André behind. Not even once did they catch sight of another human being. If it weren't for the sun pouring light into the air and onto things, and if not for the clear, sparse air, that desert and that silence would have been intolerably oppressive. So in that way, the mountain offered a kind of intimacy, a tranquil, trusting caress.

But when the sun started lowering to the horizon, and the valleys dissolved into the penumbra, and the hills and rocks cast their long shadows, and the air started to become cold and humid, then the commanding mountain gained a suddenly new grandeur and seemed to peer with hostility upon the intruders.

Almost night now, Lambaça started going down a steep slope bristling with high brush and oleaster. Forced to follow his leader, who disappeared with every step, André was walking blind, tripping, falling, colliding with bushes and getting caught in their grip, scratched and poked by dry branches and rough foliage.

Night caught up with them on the descent, and when they left the thickets and entered the bottom of the valley, everything around them was black. With a nervous, quickened gait, Lambaça strode across an open field and started climbing another slope. Worn out, with an even sharper pain in his lung, André followed him arduously, always climbing and clambering, an hour or even more. In some places walking, other places crawling, they arrived at a shelf where Lambaça stopped, breathing hard, watching and listening. Below, in front of them, complete darkness and silence. Above them, way above, the black outline of the mountains, a sash of starry, cold sky smiled protectively.

Surely Lambaça had been there many times. In the darkness, he disappeared into the earth. Following him, André found himself in a den whose soil, where they sat down, felt strangely moist and lumpy. Somewhere, water was dripping slowly, irregularly. After several long minutes, Lambaça started to smoke, carefully hiding the glow of the cigarette in the conch of his hands.

"So?" André asked, breathing with difficulty.

Lambaça took two more drags before answering. "We'll see," he said finally, drawling indifferently.

"My friend," André said, feeling his voice rise with anger, "I am not happy with your behavior. I want to know what I should be expecting. I'm not comfortable—"

"Don't get excited, don't get excited," Lambaça interrupted him disdainfully.

"—not comfortable just walking blindly. I told you that once already and I'm saying it again. Answer me clearly: When are we crossing?"

Lambaça didn't answer right away. The glow of his cigarette tinged red the joints of his fingers that held it. Once again, slowly, a solitary, cheerless drop of water fell.

"Maybe tomorrow," he answered at last in a mocking, condescending tone.

"You're messing with me, and this is not going to end well," André fired back at him angrily, without even knowing himself what he meant by such words.

Then the stub of the cigarette crumbled to the ground and went out. Soon Lambaça yawned.

"Are we spending the night here?"

"That depends," Lambaça answered with another yawn.

Irritated, tired and hungry, sitting on the ground and leaning against the wall of the den, feeling the wetness creep into his pants and the cold stone into his back, André struggled not to sleep. From time to time, he heard Lambaça rustling around at some distance and saw him light another cigarette, cautiously covering the light from the match in a corner with his coat. Afterward, the regular glow of the cigarette was concealed in the curve of his hands. Lambaça didn't sleep or make any pretense of it. What was he thinking? What was he planning? Had he brought him here to assault and rob him? André felt a growing distrust of the man. As he had done the night before on his straw bed, he instinctively felt the envelope with the money. And thus the hours passed, in silence, in the dark and cold. The uncertain, slow drip injected a note of mystery in the night.

Two more goats showed up at the entrance to the den, looking inside with the same curiosity.

Chapter 9

ANDRÉ awoke, sensing a strange presence, and saw, a few feet away, the muzzle of a curious goat spying calmly into the den. And then he heard the timid tinkle of a bell. Next to the goat there appeared a kid goat in the sunlight, looking inquisitively inside.

Leaning against the wall of the den, his arms crossed, his black hat tilted over to cover his face, Lambaça was sleeping. André woke him.

"Oh, great!" Lambaça exclaimed.

Other bells could be heard above them, disparate and uncertain, and a second goat came leaning over the den, looking nosily inside, like the first.

"Don't let them in!" Lambaça continued. "If anyone sees this scene from afar, they'll know somebody's here."

It was the first time Lambaça had offered a clear, reasonable interpretation of anything. It was also the first time André noticed some disquiet and nervousness in his voice. For one reason or another, he didn't think their situation so extraordinary.

"Should we stay?" André asked.

Lambaça seemed to regret that he had spoken so much, as though it were a sign of weakness. Without answering, he quietly began making a cigarette. Once in a while, he peered over the lip of the den from under his hat's black brim. The two goats didn't move, and from the sound of nearby bells, apparently other goats were approaching. André now looked at the nature of the ground where they had slept: tiny dark olives decomposing in the dampness. But why did the goats want to gather here by day, when they had spent the night out in the fields? This question piqued his interest. Two more goats showed up at the entrance to the den, looking inside with the same curiosity, standing with the others.

"Oh, really great, dammit!" Lambaça said again. "We have to get going."

Out there, the sun, already high, beat fully on the den's slope. Just as they had imagined, dozens of goats spread out all over the area, obviously perplexed. Only here and there a few little kids cavorted playfully. When the men appeared, the whole flock, shining in the sunlight, galloped alongside them in a sweet alarm of bells and the crush of heavy gentle bodies. Making a visor of his hands, Lambaça carefully surveyed the crest of the horizon. Then, with affected deliberation, erect body and bowed legs, his hand in his belt coddling the revolver under his coattail, he started following after the goats in a daring stride as if defying any invisible enemy who might be observing them from the other hill.

Reaching the bottom of the valley, carpeted by a growth of young weeds and vines, they started climbing up the hillside of oleaster and thickets, which the night before they had climbed down with such difficulty. If it had been hard going down, going up was an acrobatic feat. At midday, having conquered yet another steep wall of brush, which tore both his clothes and his flesh, André lost track of Lambaça and, completely exhausted, drenched in sweat, the shooting pain piercing him, he simply fell in a heap panting.

So he remained, his eyes closed, incapable of reacting or rising to his feet, until a stupor overtook him. Nestling himself into the bushes as best he could, he fell into a profound sleep. When he awoke, in the fading twilight, Lambaça was crouching beside him. Immediately he threw at him, even more cruelly, the same phrase he had offensively thrown at him the first day they had talked:

"These things are for men, my friend."

André had borne much, Lambaça knew perfectly well. He had been forced onto futile hikes, running after the jitney, sleeping badly at night, fasting for prolonged periods. Without explanation, with no discernible goals. Everything showed only disorientation and bad faith. André sat up impetuously, leaning over with his face provocatively in Lambaça's.

"We don't eat today?" he asked bitterly.

Lambaça's black eyes shone ironically. Slowly he reached his hand into his pocket and extended it open. In his palm he offered some small brown hazelnuts.

"A very poor joke!" André shouted. "What the hell are you doing? Are you crazy or what?"

Lambaça shrugged his shoulders and sighed indifferently. From his belt he drew the enormous silver revolver, raked the ground with the barrel until he found a stone, and breaking the hazelnuts open with the butt, casually started eating them. When he finished, he took out his flask of brandy and offered it to André, who refused. So Lambaça drank slowly, clicked his tongue, put the flask away, lay back the best he could and covered his face with his hat.

André was quite awake by now, with a commanding need to discuss the situation.

"Since midday yesterday, we haven't eaten anything. If we were going to be trekking so much, why didn't we bring something from the house where we were? And if we could have spent the night out here and now we had to come back, why did we lose hours and hours going all the way to the den with the goats? What did we accomplish in twenty-four hours in this valley? Do you have the least idea what you intend to do?"

His eyes ever hidden by his black hat, Lambaça yawned loudly and settled himself a little better into the shrubs.

"I don't know, and I don't even want to know what you were doing at that house. It wasn't a good thing, that's for sure. But you promised to get me over the border, and up to now, I don't see anything. I already asked you many times and I demand you give me an answer. When are we crossing?"

Lambaça remained impassive. He wasn't sleeping, because once again he yawned.

Lambaça's mute calm further infuriated André. He shouted, course and sharp, "Did you hear me? Answer! This is what I'm paying you for!"

Only then did Lambaça straighten up, uncovering his face. In the dusk, André could still see his eyes flashing with evil. The voice, however, came as always, calmly and disdainfully.

"Are you a fool, or what? Speak softly."

"Speak softly, speak softly, that's all you know how to say. You are mistaken with me. If you think you're playing a trick on me, there'll be hell to pay. I'm here for offing someone. I don't mind offing another."

"Speak softly, didn't you hear me?"

"When are we crossing?" André insisted, moderating his voice against his will. "When are we crossing? Answer! Right now!"

"Tomorrow," Lambaça responded, detached. And without caring to hear any more threats from André, he lay himself down again, as best he could among the bushes, once again pulling his hat over his face. In a few moments, even before night had completely fallen, he was snoring.

André was about to grab him and punch him awake. But he wound up nestling in, too. Only much later, already when day was dawning, the stars peeking through the thickets and a creeping chill moving over him, did he relax enough to fall asleep.

Chapter **10**

LAMBAÇA woke him up. They marched all morning, uphill and down, as if aimlessly. Famished and exhausted, André kept up only with exertion. They did not talk.

Around midday, rounding a hillock, they saw below them, just a few steps away, a dark, miserable house, similar to so many others: stone piled upon stone, thatched roof, earthen corral with the living quarters on the second floor, two crude windows without glass. They walked down a path around the house and stopped in front. On the porch, a young woman was rocking a baby. Although seeing them come out of nowhere, she looked at them with no surprise.

Lambaça did not say hello. He just asked: "Is anyone else here?"

The young woman smiled and shook her head. Lambaça slowly looked around and asked for something to eat.

"That can be arranged," the woman responded in a frail but amiable tone, smiling again and looking at André interestedly.

Hearing talk of eating thrilled the young man's heart.

But in Lambaça's black, nervous little eyes, in the way he tightened his lips under his brush of a mustache, he was visibly not content. He kept looking out far and questioningly over the mountains. Something weird was obvious in his indecisiveness and in the girl's apathetic bearing, always walking back and forth and rocking the baby.

Although nearly hidden in the shadow of the porch, the girl's figure seemed gallant and, under her modest dark kerchief, a pure, beatific smile brightened her fine features. Maybe somewhat too honest.

"Listen," Lambaça said at last, "go get Rosa and bring some wine."

To André, this request seemed sensible, because the young woman, being alone, likely wouldn't want to receive two men in the house.

"Zulmira. did you hear?" Lambaça insisted. "Or are you expecting someone?"

"No," the woman answered in the same fragile, friendly voice. After a pause, still rocking the baby, she added, "Are you staying?"

Eyeing his companion, waiting for the response, André found a new and disturbing expression. Lambaça nodded affirmatively, his little black eyes fixed mischievously on the girl, his half-open mouth showing his aggressive teeth. Something crude, abusive and mean showed in his whole affect.

"I don't know if Rosa can come," the girl said hesitantly.

"And if we stay," Lambaça asked gently, "are you afraid?"

This whole scene sparked an indefinable sourness and vague apprehension in André. He could easily see his companion, imagining the girl alone in the house, engaging in some ugly business. That man was capable of anything. What complicity would he expect of him?

Stepping away from the house a bit, he called out to Lambaça. He came.

"Do they offer room and board here?"

Lambaça kept quiet, his eyes unmoving and cruel. He started moving his lips to speak, but he said nothing. He shrugged his shoulders, turned his back and headed back to the house.

The young man jumped three steps and stopped him. "What are you planning to do?" he asked, getting more and more upset.

Lambaça shrugged his shoulders again, but this time answered in a deliberate, condescending voice that trickled coldly through his closed lips. "Calm down, friend, calm down. It's not expensive, ease up."

And he went back toward the house.

"I don't know if Rosa can stay," the girl repeated, always rocking the baby.

Once more, she looked intently at André with her simple, serene smile, and the young man felt flustered by the tenacity of that look. It recalled something to him, distant and unpleasant, but what was it, what?

"Go take care of things," said Lambaça.

The girl adjusted the child in her arms, turned to look at André and disappeared into the house.

"Does she live alone?" André asked.

Lambaça exploded with an evil, mocking laugh that again showed his teeth below that brush of a mustache. He didn't answer.

"I'm not staying here!" André declared, in a quick, involuntary decision.

"Don't stay," Lambaça said coarsely.

André grabbed his arm. The agitated words left his throat so quietly that he feared they might not be heard. "I'm not staying and neither are you!"

Without withdrawing his arm, Lambaça once again laughed derisively, his eyes fuming with hatred. For a moment, the boy had the feeling that the man might treacherously stab him in the gut.

"Fine," said Lambaça, lightly removing his arm in a slow, gentle gesture that showed off the heft of his well-built musculature. He strode to the house, walked up to the porch and entered.

André stood there alone, not knowing what to do, and waited a long time. On an unfamiliar mountain range, in a border zone, with no idea where he was, worn-out and famished—the dangers started adding up in earnest. Since he had been introduced to Lambaça, he feared it would all end badly. Several times already, he saw himself as a lost cause. Now he just found himself powerless. Did he have to bend one more time, go up to the porch, knock and call out? What would await him? Or would he humiliate Lambaça with bitter words, reminding him of promises and responsibilities? Unfortunately, he didn't even have a weapon.

Lambaça returned, though. He had stayed inside a least an hour, but he returned. He descended the stairs, slightly arching his strong legs, still eating, cleaning off his mouth and mustache with the back of his hand. Seeing the young man seated on a rock, he looked at him disparagingly. Of course he knew he'd be waiting. His whole demeanor radiated satisfaction and self-assurance.

Making a simple hand gesture, he started walking, certain the younger one would follow.

Before departing, André looked back at the porch. The girl's head appeared in the doorway, in shadow. She arranged the locks of her hair beneath her headscarf and looked at him without smiling, with an attentive, questioning air.

Lambaça strutted away, walking fast, and André almost had to run to catch up.

He raised his weapon in the direction of the youth and pulled the trigger once, twice, three times.

Chapter 11

ALL afternoon they walked through the mountains. Now Lambaça went unhurriedly, making leisurely stops. He seemed in a good mood, as if implying he had forgiven the earlier drama. Suddenly he seemed to have gained interest in the person who accompanied him, and several times, walking beside him, he surprised him by turning to look at him.

At one stop, next to a small stream of water, Lambaça pulled his big silver revolver out of his pocket, and after unloading it, started examining the hammer and lock functions. With the damp yellow end of his cigarette stuck to his lower lip, he drew deep, long inhalations of smoke.

Lambaça had said the night before that they would cross the frontier today. Could that be why he was examining his weapon? Wanting confirmation, André returned to the subject. The response was less certain than yesterday's.

"Maybe, if they don't pump us full of lead," and he shot the youngster a quick, tricky glance.

Will he think I'm afraid? Or what is he contemplating? André thought. He sensed that this man hated him, waiting for him from moment to moment to see some sign of fear or hesitation. He also felt that if he gave off such a sign, Lambaça would abandon him; and if he didn't give off a sign, if he could convince Lambaça of his bravery (and for that reason he had even invented that story of having "offed" someone), the journey would still run the risk, with this antagonism of forces, of ending in some dramatic, violent incident. He castigated himself for having acceded to his friends' opinion that he go unarmed. But Lambaça didn't know that, and watching him examine his revolver, André thought about bolstering the idea in him that he was not unarmed.

"I like my pistol better," he said, patting his jacket pocket.

"One revolver is worth more than two pistols," Lambaça said. "Pistols jam. A revolver never fails."

As if to prove his point, he raised his weapon in the direction of the youth and pulled the trigger once, twice, three times. Once, twice, three times, the hammer snapped with a hearty though meaningless click. Remembering the story of the old man and his daughter, André shuddered. Which was obviously what Lambaça intended, because he laughed out loud.

"Show me your pistol," he challenged.

No way am I going to admit being unarmed, André thought. He answered with a question.

"We're not eating today?" he asked weakly, feeling an angry tightness in his stomach.

Lambaça shot him a sneering look.

"My friend, whoever misses the train has to wait for the next one."

He had eaten in the house of the young woman. André could have also. Feeling like he was about to faint from hunger and fatigue, the young man thought maybe he had acted too fast and carelessly. Why the hell did such strong suspicions possess him about that house, with nothing to justify them? That was stupid and childish. It was now forty-eight hours since he had eaten, and if that continued, maybe he'd end up somewhere in the midst of a thicket as a nice meal for the wolves and birds. He figured the other must have guessed his thoughts.

"You didn't eat, but you will. Rest assured, tonight you will have a fine dinner and sleep in a soft, warm bed."

And again, there was that evil smile, mocking and cruel. You could presume he was trying all he could to throw his companion off course.

"Soft and warm," he repeated.

After a while, his revolver loaded now, Lambaça pressed. "So, won't you show me your pistol?"

"My friend," André answered, imitating his companion's tone of voice, "weapons aren't toys. When you need them is the time to show them."

Only then did Lambaça slowly put his revolver away.

It was getting late when they set out walking again. Mountains and more mountains, with gently rounded peaks, smooth, ashy rocks and wild, vine-covered vegetation. Mountains so desolate and so similar that André could have sworn having already passed them. Now, just at nightfall, they were crossing that high plain with no horizon. The same peacefully symmetrical rock formations, the same trails with little violet flowers, and even the same mountain, also serene and rounded, spreading out alongside them on the way. Lambaça walked laggardly.

"Are we going to sleep out in the open air again?" André inquired.

"Calm down, my friend, calm down. We're almost there."

The new and strange tone of his voice seemed to indicate that this time he wasn't being deceptive—but also that he was.

In fact, that was just it. A few hundred meters ahead, in the twilight shadows below, they saw the obscure, dark impression of a village. They descended, stumbling down a vertical incline, passing two or three huts, made a turn, went up another path carved into the side of the hill and suddenly emerged in half a dozen steps before an isolated house.

Lambaça made a slight hissing sound between his teeth. On top, on the porch, a figure appeared in the poorly lit rectangle of the door. The two men walked up the stone stairs.

They entered. A woman, with her back toward them, placed an oil lamp on a high shelf and raised the wick to provide more light. When she turned, André was dumbstruck by surprise. From under the dark old kerchief that had dropped to her shoulder, Zulmira looked at them with her pure, serene smile.

Without any excuses or explanations, Lambaça had brought him back to the same house where André did not want to stay.

Chapter 12

RIGHT off the bat, Lambaça showed himself in control of the situation. He closed the door. Then, aggressively shoving a stool up against the table, he grabbed the girl with grotesque animal power and, removing her kerchief with his teeth, kissed her neck hungrily. The girl neither reacted nor showed surprise. While he kissed her, she looked at André, quiet and submissive.

So it was his lover! A shock at first. Then calm. Better that than be witness to some violence.

The two sat at the table, facing one another. The young woman, barefoot and poorly clothed, after bringing a carafe of wine and three glasses, sat down also, purposely, it seemed, with her chair closer to André. From this close distance, she was even more beautiful. Upon her thin, fine face, her pale, scalloped mouth smiled with purity, and her eyes, edged with long eyelashes, looked tenderly at the boy from beneath her thick eyebrows. Her kerchief once again had fallen on her shoulder, showing her full, wavy black hair gathered behind her ears in a tuft. How could it be that such a young and beautiful girl would be the lover of that man?

"Rosa's not coming," she said in a friendly but veiled voice. And she looked at one man, then the other.

Lambaça told her to get dinner and, as the woman headed to a corner, he got up, took off his jacket and placed it on a cot. Before returning to the table he went over to the girl and once again grabbed her in a loutish embrace.

She chased him away peevishly. "Don't be in such a rush, man, wait!"

And she turned to look at the young man in the corner. There was an ineffable contrast between her condescension and the purity of her features and her smile. When Lambaça came back to the table, she rearranged her headscarf, fixed her eyes on André and raised her arms gently and graciously, as if to provide enough time for him to appreciate her perfect bust. The boy felt sad, but didn't know why.

At last an enormous rye bread and a pan of eggs and sausage came to the table. The three ate from it. With his sleeves rolled up and his black hat balanced on the back of his head, Lambaça looked happy and at ease, as though in his own home. With a knife, he cut off enormous angles of bread, stuffing them into his mouth, mixed with the frittata. He drank glass after glass like a creature without a soul. André also ate with a good appetite—he had waited long for this meal—but he felt constrained, wanting this all to be over soon. The young woman nibbled at her food with delicate, timid movements, only at long intervals drinking little sips, barely touching the glass to her clear pink, moistened lips. André caught Lambaça putting his arm under the table, and occasionally the girl did the same. He saw that once she freed her body from his impertinence, she would casually and calmly rearrange her clothing. Each time he would get even sadder at her passivity, in such contrast to the delicateness of her figure. She kept looking at the young man, perhaps taken aback by his youth. More than once, freeing herself from Lambaça's touch, she drew her stool and her body closer to André, gazing at him warmly and lovingly. Her preference for André was so obvious that he began to fear an explosion from Lambaça. But no. In his little black eyes, there was no hate or animosity to be seen. Only a crude happiness.

The dinner was interrupted by the baby's crying. The young woman got up and disappeared through a dark little door. She reappeared before long with the child in her arms.

"The father?" André asked Lambaça in a low voice.

Already fairly inebriated, he let loose a metallic guffaw, wounding his companion. The woman noticed. She blushed, and for the first time, shame and embarrassment crossed her face. His question was completely idiotic.

As she sat next to the men, with her son in her arms, André saw that under her shawl she searched for and took out her breast, and he heard, following the final burst of the baby's crying, the ravenous cooing of the little mouth finding the nipple. The girl looked inside her shawl and once again her face shone with that same serene, pure smile.

With burning eyes, Lambaça cautiously placed his hand on her shoulder to caress her. Then, in a rough move, he yanked away the shawl. The girl covered herself right away.

"Brute!" she shouted angrily, rising and moving her seat next to André.

His mouth half open and stuffed with food, Lambaça looked at the young man wickedly. The boy felt that surely, step by step, the moment for some violent scene was upon him.

"How old is the baby?" he asked.

"Six months," the girl answered sweetly, with her head bent over in the shadow of the shawl and the headscarf. Then she raised her head, drew her stool even closer to André, until she was next to him and almost with her back toward Lambaça. She looked lengthily at the young man as if to say something with her eyes that he could not see. Assuredly, on top of the table and well within sight, she placed her dark hand on top of the boy's, squeezed it and let it remain there.

André believed Lambaça would stand up and start a fight with knives and guns. But it was worse, much worse than that. Only one sentence came out of his mouth, directed to the girl, but what a sentence!

"If you want, you can do him first, but you're spending the night with me."

Like a lightning bolt, that sentence illuminated everything— all that was confusing, oppressive, anguished that the lad had been feeling since they had arrived at the house earlier that day. The girl was not even Lambaça's lover. She was merely a prostitute. There, only a hundred meters from the tiny village in the middle of the mountains, in the desert.

The girl said goodbye with her hand, in a gesture so sad and forlorn; he would never stop thinking about it.

Chapter 13

FOR a few moments, he felt the desire to flee from that house and get lost in the pure mountain air. Later on, he would not be able to recall the words he had said. He would only remember having made clear that he wanted nothing from the girl, and that even if his attitude were motivated by indignation, sympathy and pity, the girl saw it only as contempt. He would remember that the girl did not want to go with Lambaça to her room, on the other side of the doorway in the back, before André had wrapped himself in the blanket on the cot in the corner. He remembered that she didn't smile any more, nor look him in the eye again. And later he'd remember, already in bed with the light out, the spiteful creaking of the bed on the other side of the partition and the muffled jolts of Lambaça's grunts.

Rolled up in the blanket, his outrage and sadness smothered him. Why was that? Why? What tragedy was hidden in that little peasant cottage a hundred meters away from a forgotten settlement in the mountains? How was that possible there? A country girl, so young, so pretty, born not to sell her love but to be loved? Whom he would be capable of loving, he was sure of it. Later, much later, André still recalled her peaceful, pure smile and would feel the sweet caress of her eyes, lined with black eyelashes, spreading out under her long, shining eyebrows. Maybe in that moment, with the ardor of his eighteen years, he was already in love. Maybe. The fact was that he felt disgusted and hopeless, as though a beloved person had been abducted from him and degraded.

Happily, Lambaça fell asleep quickly. Silence descended upon the house. Then the boy grew calm and thought about his life and the reasons why he found himself in those mountains.

He comforted himself. In the end, he was dedicating his life, joining his weakness to the millions of other weaknesses, trying to prevent the existence of girls in his country with that kind of fate. Desperately he grasped that train of thought, trying to forget the place where he was, forget Zulmira above all, her smile and her eyes, and the baby, and Lambaça, and the bed from which only a partition separated him. Tired as he was, he fell asleep.

He awakened to the light in the room. Seated at the end of the table, Zulmira was suckling her son. She was dressed, and André gladly thought maybe she had slept dressed with Lambaça. Now without her headscarf, her black hair unfurled almost to her shoulders. She freely gave of her dark, full and perfect breast. André watched for a few seconds from underneath his heavy eyelids, then fell asleep again. He woke up again not long after. She still held her son in her arms and was looking toward his corner with an earnest, worried expression. He saw her stand up, place her son in a basket, cover him, and uncertainly approach his own cot, nestling the blanket around his legs just as she had for her son. She stayed standing a few minutes and then went to sit at the table, lowering the light until it was barely a faint shadow and, crossing her arms, lay her head on them, turning it sadly from side to side a few times.

It was five o'clock, and Lambaça had said they would leave at dawn. André made himself a cigarette. As the smoke spread through the room, the girl sat upright, turned in his direction in one sudden move, and then assumed her earlier position. She was clearly wide awake. André got up and raised the wick on the oil lamp. The light gradually filled the little room. The girl didn't move. The idea that she had spent the whole night bent over the table just to avoid contact with Lambaça, in that posture of lonely abandonment, gave the young man the desire to simply, lovingly touch her resting head. But he didn't do it, and all his life he regretted not having done so. Better than he knew at the time, he later understood that the girl needed, absolutely needed, that gesture.

He went out. In the open air, the eastern sky was clearing. When he went back inside, the girl, again with her kerchief, was fanning the stove. She pretended not to see him and answered his good morning greeting in a weak voice without turning her head.

Lambaça appeared a little later. He hadn't noticed the girl's escape, or made out as if he hadn't. He sat at the table, his hat tilted over his eyes, sleepy and silent.

The young woman served coffee. André tried to see her face, searching out her tender glance and smile. But her face was hidden in the shade of her kerchief, avoiding both men. As she brought the meal for the road of bread with fried eggs to the table, a yawning Lambaça stretched his hand out to her waist to say something to her. She freed herself indelicately and retired for a few minutes to her room at the back. The young man guessed that she had gone to cry, but he never got to see her eyes when she came back out. When Lambaça, still sleepy and slow, wanted to settle his accounts, she continued fussing with things as if she didn't hear him, and only after a while, from the corner and with her back towards them, she murmured, "Put it there."

Lambaça insisted on knowing how much he owed her. In her fragile, kind voice, and still without looking at them, she finally said, "You all can pay what you think is right."

The use of the plural, the delicacy it conveyed, her whole attitude during the night and now in the early morning— everything enhanced the young man's tender and pitiful feelings. He himself felt profoundly discontented. He needed her to look at him, so that she might comprehend or guess his behavior and his sentiments. Zulmira, however, kept to her corner, killing time until the men left. Without facing them, in a weak voice, she just said some word that the young man did not understand.

Halfway down the stone steps, André stopped and turned around toward the porch. Only then, by the ashen light of morning, did he see, in Zulmira's fine countenance, her eyes directed pointedly and seriously toward him. The girl then said goodbye with her hand, in a gesture so sad and forlorn, that he would never stop thinking about it, nor ever stop feeling its pain.

Knowingly working the oars with his bony, gangly arms, he took the two men to the other side.

Chapter 14

ON a low plateau circled by sky, Lambaça sat down and unwrapped the snack package. The sun at high noon cut through the buoyant air like a hot whip. His skin glowing with sweat, Lambaça removed his jacket and slowly rolled his shirt-sleeves up the length of his hairy, sinewy arms. André did the same.

They ate hungrily, using a switchblade to cut off big slices, carefully pinching the yellow fragments of fried egg that had fallen from the bread to the paper as greasy crumbs. In a few minutes, the enormous lunch was reduced to half. Lambaça didn't stop. He continued to stuff his mouth, washing it down from time to time with gulps from his flask of brandy. Seeing that at that rate there would soon be nothing left, André remembered his hunger of the last few days.

"Wouldn't it be better to save the rest for later?" he said. "Or will we be eating dinner somewhere?"

His mouth full, Lambaça stared at his companion with those piercing little black eyes and, as his only response, cut himself another slice.

"You really could make a saint lose his patience," André insisted. "Don't you hear what I say?"

Eventually, Lambaça stopped chomping, turning and masticating his food well with violent rotations of his jaws, which brought into relief the muscles beneath his skin. He swallowed three times, and only then spoke in a sneering timbre.

"Don't worry, friend. We already crossed."

"We already crossed what?" André asked, furiously at the sneering tone.

Lambaça shrugged his shoulders and crammed his mouth again with food.

"You should be ashamed of yourself!" André spat out.

The little black eyes responded with a fleeting burst of anger. "Why all the noise?" he asked after swallowing. "I only said we already crossed," and let out a provocative peal of laughter.

"This is nothing to kid around about!" said André.

"Believe it or don't believe it, I don't care."

And Lambaça started picking at the paper with his fingertips, eagerly lifting to his tongue a few fallen morsels of egg.

André doubted it. If what Lambaça said was true, it would have happened that morning, after leaving the young woman's house. But when? He tried to recall the hike, searching for some detail along the way, or some gesture or expression from his companion that would have confirmed leaving Portugal and entering Spain.

"I didn't see anything," he said quietly, as though talking to himself.

This time, Lambaça didn't pause to swallow before speaking. With his mouth still full, his mumbled words stumbled out excitedly.

"So what did my friend expect? A wall at the frontier, huh? Or maybe a plaque?"

Unable to contain himself any longer, he exploded with renewed laughter, which sent white and yellow particles flying in all directions. Then, as if the hilarity had prevented him from eating any more, he wrapped up the rest, took another swallow, stood up and started rolling down his shirtsleeves and adjusting the cuffs.

André stood up, too. He gripped one of Lambaça's arms before they got on their way and spoke calmly: "It would have been much better if you weren't so ornery. You know why I had to leave Portugal, and you're obviously not blind to the importance of this trip. So why do you behave this way?"

"We already crossed," Lambaça simply repeated, his face suddenly shadowed by concern.

In a mere couple of hundred meters, they unexpectedly encountered a long valley with a river that eddied around little sandy islets.

"Ohhhhh!" Lambaça shouted.

"Ohhhhh!" came the echo from the other side.

Then, amongst the rushes and willows, they saw a little boat. With a dozen oar strokes it crossed the river.

"*Buenas.* Good afternoon," said the boatman in a hushed voice.

André jumped at that word. Lambaça had told the truth. They were in Spain.

"*Buenas,*" Lambaça responded.

The boatman was a skeletal old man in tatters, with a large hat pulled down over his quiet face. His deep-set, deathly eyes hardly settled on the newcomers and swung slowly and indifferently over the river and its margins.

He made no remark, nor showed any curiosity or surprise. Silently, seated aslant across the bench, knowingly working the oars with his bony, gangly arms, he took the two men to the other side. When Lambaça paid him, he received the money in the leathery palm of his hand, all the while distractedly watching the water in the river.

Lambaça ahead, André behind, they trudged another few kilometers through rough vegetation. Once they left the valley, the landscape returned to that of before—the same loneliness, the same sad, rounded hilltops and even, in the distance, that same big mountain, silent and commanding, spreading out and observing from afar.

At dusk, they staggered along a footpath that led gently down a hillside. In front and below them, in a bluish haze, they found the valley again, but now in contrast to the monotonous desolation of the mountains they had just crossed, they could discern the warm presence of human activity. In apparent scattered disorder, trees, both tall and low, slender and leafy, stood in distinct groupings, wrapped in a slight mist. The land looked planned, delineated, shorn, in a long, melancholy patchwork, peacefully arranged throughout the meadow alongside the dark line of the river, and then extending irregularly and awkwardly halfway up the mountains on the other side. In another kilometer or so, if that, a sizable village beckoned, reflecting the last rays of the sun with dazzling, twinkling lights.

Just below, already twilight, they entered upon a proper, paved road. There was something weird about finding such a road after several days of marching through desert mountains. That little highway announced the presence of both friend and foe, nourishment and danger, community and shock, all the excitement of life in human society. Lambaça halted and turned to face André. His little black eyes, under the shadow of his hat, shone maliciously.

"It's time to settle our account," André said, anticipating his guide. And he drew out the envelope from his inner pocket, bashful for some reason.

"For the crossing, two thousand. How much do I owe you for the expenses along the way?"

Lambaça almost choked on his crude laughter, as if he had been waiting a long time for those words to amuse him. Without saying anything, he pointed down the road.

"Stay on this road. Up ahead you'll find the city. Right away, to the left, you'll see the station. You don't have to ask, you can't miss it. Just buy a ticket to Madrid. Or wherever you want."

André started counting the money.

"Don't be afraid," Lambaça added, in his disdainful, annoying voice. "We're pretty far from the border, and security is weak here."

"So, how much for the other expenses?" André demanded.

"Pay what you think is right," Lambaça answered, imitating Zulmira's voice when they left her.

These words scorched the young man, reopening the wound. Maybe just for that reason Lambaça said them.

"How much?"

Lambaça didn't answer.

"Two hundred escudos more, is that good?" asked André, counting out bills. "Two hundred and fifty?"

Silence.

"So?"

Lambaça turned his back and walked half a dozen steps in the other direction from where he had pointed. André thought he had remained close by to take care of some need.

"So?" he repeated.

Without answering or turning around, Lambaça kept walking away on the road.

"Hey!" André shouted.

Lambaça, with his arched legs, his torso erect in his plain black suit, walked on with his measured bold gait.

"Hey!!" an irritated André shouted again.

There was something he only realized now, and felt the sudden, imperative need to say.

"Yaaaaay!!!"

In the fading light of the falling night, Lambaça's figure disappeared around the first bend in the road.

André tucked his money away and strode off in the opposite direction.

A Short Biographical Note on the Author

Manuel Tiago

Manuel Tiago was the pen name of Álvaro Cunhal. Edições Avante! in Lisbon, has published six titles by Manuel Tiago: *Até Amanhã, Camaradas* (Until Tomorrow, Comrades), which was adapted as a Portuguese television series in 2005; *A Estrela de Seis Pontas* (The Six-Pointed Star); *A Casa de Eulália* (The House of Eulália); *Fronteiras* (Frontiers); *Um Risco na Areia* (A Mark in the Sand); and *Cinco Dias, Cinco Noites* (Five Days, Five Nights), adapted to film in 1996. This is the first of his works of fiction to appear in English.

Álvaro Cunhal was born in Coimbra, Portugal, on November 9, 1913. He began his revolutionary activity as a student at the law school (Faculdade de Direito) of Lisbon. He participated in the student movement and was elected in 1934 as the student representative to the University Senate. He was a militant in the Federation of Portuguese Communist Youth (Federação da Juventude Comunista Portuguesa), and was elected its secretary-general in 1935. In that year he went underground and participated in Moscow in the Sixth

International Communist Youth Congress. He joined the Portuguese Communist Party (Partido Comunista Português, PCP) in 1931.

Arrested in 1937 and 1940, and subjected to torture, he returned to political struggle as soon as he was freed after several months in prison. He participated in the reorganization of the PCP in 1940-41. Again living clandestinely, he was a member of the party Secretariat from 1942 to 1949.

Arrested anew in 1949 and brought before a fascist court, he delivered a ringing denunciation of the fascist dictatorship and a defense of his party's program. Judged guilty, he remained for 11 years in fascist prisons, almost eight of them in complete isolation. On January 3, 1960, he escaped from the prison fortress at Peniche together with a group of brave communist militants. Once again called to the Secretariat of the Central Committee, he was elected Secretary General of the PCP in 1961.

Living abroad, in Moscow and Paris, from that time forward he participated in numerous congresses and gatherings with communist parties and other revolutionary forces in international conferences. He played a critical role in organizing worldwide support, especially within the socialist countries, for the independence movements in the far-flung Portuguese colonies in Africa.

After the downfall of the fascist dictatorship on April 25, 1974, he served as Minister without Portfolio in the first, second, third and fourth provisional governments, and was elected as a deputy to the Constituent Assembly in 1975 and to the Assembly for the Republic in 1975, 1979, 1980, 1983, 1985 and 1987. He was a member of the Council of State from 1982 to 1992.

In accordance with the decisions made at the Fourteenth Congress of the PCP in 1992 concerning renewal and a new structure of leadership, he stepped down as Secretary General of the PCP and was elected by the Central Committee as President of the National Council of the party.

In December 1996, the Fifteenth Congress of the PCP eliminated the National Council of the party and its presidency. Cunhal was re-elected as a member of the Central Committee.

He was re-elected to the Central Committee at the Sixteenth and Seventeenth party congresses in December 2000 and November 2004 respectively.

Under his own name Cunhal published several books about politics. He was a gifted artist as well: A book of his collected drawings has appeared. In addition, he published an original translation of Shakespeare's *King Lear*.

He died at the age of 91 on June 13, 2005. His funeral in Lisbon was attended by half a million people. He had one daughter, Ana Cunhal.

Photo: Fernando Pereira

About the Translator

Eric A. Gordon, a Los Angeles resident since 1990, is a native of New Haven, Connecticut. His undergraduate degree is from Yale University, where he majored in Latin American Studies. He studied Spanish five years and Portuguese two years. He also took a summer residency in Portuguese at New York University. He went on to Tulane University, where he continued studying Portuguese and wrote a master's thesis on the opera in Rio de Janeiro in the 19th century, using original sources uncovered in the Arquivo Nacional. He earned a doctorate in history, also from Tulane, writing his dissertation about the anarchist movement in Brazil in the pre-World War I era. He also studied Portuguese language and culture under a Gulbenkian Foundation fellowship in Lisbon.

Gordon is the author of *Mark the Music: The Life and Work of Marc Blitzstein*, and co-author of *Ballad of an American: The Autobiography of Earl Robinson*. A memoir in short story form that he translated from Portuguese, *Waving to the Train and Other Stories*, by Hadasa Cytrynowicz, appeared in 2013 from Blue Thread Press. In 2015 he executive produced the compact disk *City of the Future: Yiddish Songs from the Former Soviet Union*, a collection of songs composed in 1931 by Samuel Polonski to the lyrics of major Soviet Yiddish poets. He is the author of a currently unpublished political autobiography.

From 1995 to 2010, Gordon was Director of the Workmen's Circle/Arbeter Ring in Southern California. He previously worked at Social and Public Art Resource Center, helping to produce murals all around the city of Los Angeles, which gave him the experience to commission a mural at the Workmen's Circle building. He was Southern California Chapter Chair of the National Writers Union (Local 1981 UAW/AFL-CIO) for two terms. He has written for dozens of local, national, and international publications, mostly about art, music, culture, and politics. From 2014 onward, he has been a staff writer and editor for *People's World* online newspaper.

From 2006-09 Gordon took coursework toward certification as a Secular Jewish Leader, referred to in Yiddish as a *veg-vayzer*. Upon graduation, he became a legal officiant certified to conduct weddings and other ceremonial functions, a role equivalent in law to a minister, priest, or rabbi. He has a similar endorsement as a Humanist celebrant for people of any background. For five years he served as a Deputy Commissioner of Civil Marriage for the County of Los Angeles, where he conducted 1500 marriages.

Eric A. Gordon can be contacted at ericarthurgo@gmail.com.

About the Illustrator

Artist Ilse Gordon lives in Cos Cob, Connecticut, where she is known for her local landscapes of public parks and private gardens. A graduate of Sarah Lawrence College, she continued her studies at the Art Students' League and The National Academy of Design. Her work can be found in both private and public collections, including in the permanent collection of Greenwich Library's Main Branch. *Greenwich Magazine* featured one of her paintings on its cover. Beyond drawing, painting and printmaking, she also creates three-dimensional art, making numerous screens and tiled and painted furniture. Her website is www.ilsegordon.com.

Some Questions to Ponder and Discuss

From whose point of view is the story told? Why do you think so, and why did the author make that choice?

The author depicts two complex individuals at different stages of their lives. What are the positive and the negative features of each of the men?

Do the characters seem real and believable? Can you relate to their predicaments? To what extent do they remind you of yourself or someone you know?

What do you think of the way women characters are portrayed?

Even the minor characters, such as Zulmira or the old man with the rambling story, or the two women in the first house, are vividly drawn. What's the significance of their inclusion in this story?

What are the major conflicts in the story?

Do you believe this story had to take five days, five nights? Why was this title chosen for the book?

The story clearly takes place in Portugal during an oppressive time. But many details are purposefully obscure, such as the specific time period in which it happened, what route they took to the border and where they crossed it, etc. What are your thoughts about these things?

Do you think the author was intentionally trying to create a "film noir" sensibility echoing the dark pessimism of that esthetic from the 1940s?

In what genre of fiction would you classify this novella?

A novella is a long short story, not meant to capture the full atmosphere and range of experience, nor the larger and more developed cast of characters that a novel might contain. Did you miss any pieces of information that you feel you needed, and why?

Did you feel that the illustrations helped you imagine the scenes the author described, or were they unnecessary?

Did the ending surprise you?

Was it useful to read the author's biography?

Do the events in the book reveal evidence of the author's world view?

What did you learn from reading this book?

Imagining a sequel to this book, what do you think would happen to the characters?

CPSIA information can be obtained
at www.ICGtesting.com
Printed in the USA
BVHW071623231222
654910BV00001B/138